WITHDRAWN

DATE DUE			

NP
20X/7/96

E   McAllister,
McA   Angela
      Christmas wish

For my mother with all my love
from Angela Jane

For Kath, the little girl who watched with wonder
the snow from her window on Windsor Bank,
And for Clunie who has yet to discover
the magic of Christmas
S J-P

VIKING
Published by the Penguin Group
Viking Penguin, a division of Penguin Books USA Inc.,
375 Hudson Street, New York, New York 10014, U.S.A.
Penguin Books Australia Ltd, Ringwood, Victoria, Australia
Penguin Books Canada Ltd, 2801 John Street, Markham, Ontario, Canada L3R 1B4
Penguin Books (N.Z.) Ltd, 182-190 Wairau Road, Auckland 10, New Zealand

First published 1990 in Great Britain by ABC, All Books for Children,
a division of The All Children's Company Ltd,
First American edition published in 1991

1   3   5   7   9   10   8   6   4   2

Text copyright © 1990 Angela McAllister
Illustrations copyright © 1990 Susie Jenkin-Pearce

Library of Congress Catalog Card Number 50262

ISBN 0-670-84107-2

Printed and bound in Hong Kong

The
Christmas Wish

Story by

Angela McAllister

Illustrations by

Susie Jenkin-Pearce

Viking

It was the night before Christmas. In the market square, a giant fir tree had been decorated with wooden toys, and a fairy had been set on top to watch over the little town.

The shop windows had been dressed with garlands and cherubs.

The churchyard crib had been scattered with straw. Painted figures gazed at the empty manger where the baby would lie.

Full of hope, the children had hung up their empty stockings and left a mince pie and a glass of milk for Santa Claus.

And in the gardens, snowmen and snow babies pulled their scarves a little tighter against the chilly night air.

Everything in the little town was ready.

Everybody was asleep ... everybody except Tilly, who stared up at the night sky, tingling with excitement.

Suddenly, a shooting star danced right over the moon. Tilly made a wish and waited, but not a snowflake stirred. She wished again, harder, but the snow-hush was deeper than silence.

Then, slowly, a brighter star arose to outshine every other and Tilly wished a third time. At once, a tiny silver flash danced across the sky, with a faint tinkle of bells. It twisted, swaying and swerving, nearer and nearer.

Tilly held her breath — and then she gasped!

Over the rooftops galloped nine reindeer pulling
a sleigh, wildly out of control. And there was Santa
with one hand over his eyes, holding on for all he
was worth!

The sleigh crash-landed in the vegetable patches
and Santa tumbled out, and rolled with a bump to
Tilly's back door.

Tilly crept downstairs and peeped out the door to
see Santa brushing the snowflakes from his whiskers.

"So, it was *your* wish that set my reindeer a-dithering,"
he said merrily, with a wink. "A wish on the Christmas
Star is a mighty magical thing. Well, here I am! But
now I shall need your help, Mathilda of midnight
miracles, to deliver all these presents!"

The reindeer nibbled the holly hedge unhelpfully,
as Tilly gazed at the scattered presents.

Santa called them all by name — "Dasher, Dancer,
Prancer, and Vixen, Comet, Cupid, Donner, and Blitzen....

Rudolf, chief mischief-maker — come out wherever
you are!" With one great leap, Rudolf, who had been
hiding behind the chimney, jumped down into the garden.

Santa sent Rudolf to find
more helping hands while he and Tilly
gathered up all the presents. As she hunted
in the shadows of the holly hedge, she
thought she heard the wind whisper her name…
"Tilly, Tilly, open the garden gate…"
Curious, Tilly pushed open the gate. There,
to her astonishment, were all the snow babies
come to help Santa!
    As they shuffled in, Rudolf returned in a proud
gallop. Behind him flew the fairy from the Christmas
tree, the cherubs in their garlands, the crib angels with
their golden horns, and a dozen wooden soldiers leading
all the toys from the market square.

Santa welcomed them all and gave each one a sack of presents. The snow babies climbed on to the reindeers' backs, while Tilly rode Rudolf himself, galloping, galloping up into the starry night sky.

Rudolf landed silently on the rooftops and Tilly crept through open windows. Tiptoeing through the houses, Tilly left a Christmas present for every child who had been good, and slipped the mince pie that had been left for Santa into her dressing-gown pocket.

Anyone who had woken on
that Christmas Eve night and
seen reindeer, snow babies,
and cherubs flying in the starlight
laden with presents, would have
thought they were still dreaming.

Meanwhile, in Tilly's garden, Santa had just finished fixing his broken sleigh, when he heard a tinkling of bells.

Santa's helpers had returned. He was so delighted that the presents had been delivered that he decided they should all have a midnight feast. So, quiet as mice, the snow babies, the soldiers, and all the wooden toys crept upstairs to Tilly's bedroom, while the Christmas fairy, cherubs, and crib angels flew in through the window. If the cherubs sat on the bookshelf there was just enough room for everybody. Tilly emptied the pies from her pocket and climbed on to Santa's lap. As they all ate mince pies by the light of the moon, he whispered stories about the North Pole.

Suddenly, the church clock struck midnight. With a yawn, the Christmas fairy said it was time to go. When everyone had said goodbye, Santa pulled a present with torn wrapping from his pocket.

"What shall we do with this extra one?" he asked,
with a twinkle in his eye.

Tilly looked at the baby doll's face peeping through
the paper and she whispered in Santa's ear.

Hand in hand, they walked to the church crib.
Gently, Tilly lay the baby in the manger and, high
in the night sky, the Christmas Star blinked brightly.
Now Christmas had truly begun!

When they returned to Tilly's garden, they found
Dasher, Dancer, Prancer, and Vixen, Comet, Cupid,
Donner, and Blitzen, and Rudolf snuggled fast asleep.

"Up and away!" called Santa. "Our night's
work is done."
Sleepy Tilly kissed Santa goodnight.

From inside, Tilly watched the silver sleigh disappear beyond the moon. She climbed into bed and there, on her pillow, she found the wand with the golden star — just like the star she had wished on that very Christmas night.